I0551544

The Last Days of
Benjamin Constant

The Last Days of
Benjamin Constant

A Historical Novella

Jorge Pinto Mazal

Jorge Pinto Books, Inc.
Washington DC

The Last Days of Benjamin Constant: A Historical Novella

Copyright © 2024 by Jorge Pinto Mazal

ISBN: 979-8-9909299-0-6

Edition Charles King (www.ckmm.com)

Contents

A Note on the Text

This novella is not a biographical essay or a biography; it is mostly fiction. It can be listed under the category of historical novel since the main protagonist, Benjamin Constant, was a relevant thinker during the French Revolution and a well-known author on legal and political issues, along with the classic novella *Adolphe*. This text includes details of his unique character and personal and political life, as well as the realities of the tumultuous era in which he lived. The friends, family, foes, lovers, wives, and other characters included in the text are real, including their names and relationships. Most of them played an important role during the Revolution.

Dates and events may not always be entirely accurate or complete since the focus is not on providing a detailed timeline or history, but on highlighting Benjamin Constant's significant role as a staunch advocate of individual freedom. His ideas remain relevant beyond his era and can be applied to contemporary times. For instance, Isaiah Berlin, a highly influential philosopher, credited Benjamin Constant as a major influence on his theoretical thinking.

Biographical historical fiction, or *biofiction*, is different. A title and contents can be named and related to a real-life person, but the protagonist's character, dates, places, and situations can be partly fictional and arbitrary, the product of an author's imagination. An author is free to invent details for a life that may or may not have a relationship with reality.

For those interested in learning about these types of literature, I recommend reading *"Biofiction: An Introduction"* by Michael Lackey, which inspired me to venture into and explore this writing genre.

Today

After a life filled with adventure in politics and love, I find myself growing old and lonely. Nowadays, love and romance seem distant. I have lost my charm, looks, and desire, as is expected with age. Seated in my studio, surrounded by books, objects, and portraits of ancestors and admired friends, framed in diverse styles, I can reflect on my life. I can do this just by looking at my walls and bookcase filled with journals and pamphlet covers depicting various moments of the Revolution. Surrounded by this rich material, full of experiences, I can write my story. My story was part of the Revolution with all its twists and turns. I cannot help but think about the erratic part of my life. I must admit that, as my dear friends and enemies saw me, I lived with conflicting tendencies, adapting to the political circumstances of my turbulent time. Yet, I have survived, and here I am in my studio, contemplating what to do with my remaining years. I am determined to write one last book, demonstrating that all those fluctuations had a common purpose: to find a government that can ensure individual freedom and minimize the harmful influence of autocrats and ignorant crowds.

It is getting late as I observe the pink and purple hues of the sky reflected in the glass objects in my window. I am certain that the sunset was magnificent, as they often are during the winter season here in Paris.

I am deeply indebted to the English culture and my mentors during my youth in Scotland and Oxford. However, the key to becoming the person I am today is owed to my extraordinary lovers and friends, namely Isabelle de Charrière, Madame Récamier, and particularly Germaine de Staël, whose departure from this world I still mourn, even though it has been almost ten years.

I was educated in their salons, surrounded by their lovers and intellectual friends, absorbing their sense of humor, their passions, and their ideas. I miss them all. Through these experiences, I learned to argue and express my evolving ideas over time. Unfortunately, I have acquired many enemies who dislike me, particularly for my thoughts. Even now, after being politically involved during the turbulent times in France, I continue to face challenges from those who question my right to be considered a Frenchman, even after thirty years of residence.

At this stage of my life, I have no reason to complain, especially now that the end feels so near. During a deeply emotional conversation after dinner, my wise friend Germaine, shortly before her passing, shared her insight with me. Seated in front of the fireplace, sipping Cognac in her chateaux in Coppet, she said, "As we grow older, we find ourselves living in the past, as there is little future left."

Today, I vividly recollect the moment when I found myself seated near her in the bedroom, observing her weariness and diminishing strength, akin to a flickering flame gradually fading like a dying candle. It evoked memories of the numerous moments we shared together in our youth, when we were both ardently involved in political activism, engaging in impassioned discussions about human rights, recounting our respective romantic encounters, reflecting on our writings, and above all, cherishing our shared devotion to individual freedom.

Meeting Germaine de Staël on the road to Coppet in Switzerland and riding with her in her carriage was an unforgettable experience in my life. She was an incredibly influential woman in Europe, known for her close friendships with prominent intellectuals of the time, including Lafayette and Condorcet. I was immediately drawn to her, not only because of her captivating appearance, but primarily because of her brilliant ideas, particularly her unwavering commitment to individual freedom and her courageous efforts in aiding numerous French intellectuals and political figures in escaping the chaos and terror brought about by the Revolution in France. Encountering Germaine took place during one of the darkest periods of my life, following the revolutionary upheaval in France, which stripped away any sense of freedom or security that I had previously enjoyed. In those tumultuous years of madness, with mobs pillaging Paris and the heads of once respected nobility (including the Royal Family) gruesomely displayed in public squares amidst cheering crowds, terror was vividly demonstrated in the destructive power of demagogues who imposed countless decrees and death sentences upon former colleagues whose only crime was to hold differing opinions.

My unwavering commitment to individual freedom, which has guided my life, can be attributed to the distressing experiences I have endured. For four decades, I have staunchly defended the same principle: the unrestricted liberty of individuals in all aspects of life, encompassing religion, philosophy, literature, industry, and politics. By freedom, I refer to the triumph of the individual both over despotic authorities seeking to govern, and over the masses who seek to subordinate minorities to majorities. I have always acknowledged the origins of my convictions and the profound influence of England on many of my political ideas, particularly the concept of a stable and tolerant parliamentary system of governance. This notion has often caused tension between myself and my French peers and adversaries throughout the ever-changing political regimes and stages I have been fortunate to be a part of.

There are numerous connections and points of interest that I shared with Germaine, who, like me, also had friends and enjoyed the same experience of living in

England. In January 1793, she joined the controversial exiled Comte de Narbonne, who is likely the father of her son. This occurred during a time of war between England and France, which made her trip a scandal of greater magnitude.

I am aware of the criticism regarding the alleged lack of consistency and the various turns in my relationship with Napoleon Bonaparte's different regimes. This includes opposing him in 1799 and later assisting in the drafting of a constitution that ensured some form of freedom and popular representation.

Germaine probably never forgave me for welcoming Napoleon when he returned to France after escaping from Elba. She had good reasons to hate him and all that he represented. I, too, disliked his actions and lack of education. She rightly compared him to the austere Jacobin who led the Terror of 1793–1794, a "Robespierre on horseback."

I always recall the wars that Napoleon led, where countless lives were lost and an insatiable thirst for power prevailed. There were valid reasons to despise him, as he was a dictator and an autocrat. Dear Germaine, you and I had to depart from Paris, forced into exile because of him. This brings me back to our final days together, perhaps months before your passing, when I questioned why Napoleon, at the pinnacle of his power, was so afraid of you and refused to meet with you to reconcile, despite your remarkable talents. After all, he had exploited mine. Undoubtedly, Napoleon regarded you as a threat, and he was correct in doing so. Your connections and wisdom posed a danger, and he was well aware of it. And yes, my dearest friend, if you can hear me from heaven, I admit that I erred in aligning myself with that man. However, it was not the man himself, but rather the opportunity to contribute to the establishment of laws and institutions, an entire constitution. That is why I agreed to work for that ambitious and detestable individual, back during the 100 days. I sought validation for myself, even if you never approved, believing it was my duty to legislate not for the autocrat, but for individual freedom and the betterment of France.

Germaine, we worked together to create pamphlets expressing our opposition towards him, accurately labeling him as a barbarian. He wasn't just a barbarian, but also a usurper who relied solely on perpetual warfare until his demise in a final battle with a devastating defeat. As I have tried to explain on multiple occasions, he tempted me with his idea of him wanting to become a constitutional monarch, which aligned with my own desire to establish regulations that would limit authority—his and those who will succeed him, as protectors of the fundamental rights that hold great value for us.

In my esteemed project, the noble objective was to adapt, modernize, and curtail the authority of the Monarchy through the establishment of a popular assembly that governed. The booklet that lies before me encompasses the entirety of this concept. It came to light a few days prior to the Charter of 1814, bearing the title *Réflexions sur les Constitutions, la distribution des pouvoirs et les garanties dans une Monarchie constitutionnelle* (Reflections on Constitutions, the Distribution of Powers, and Safeguards in a Constitutional Monarchy). Subsequently, it took on a more refined form as the *Principes de Politique applicable à tous les Gouvernements représentatifs* (Principles of Politics Applicable to All Representative Governments). It is indeed true that this work served as a constitutional justification for Napoleon's "Empire of the Hundred Days".

I am well aware of my arguable non-French heritage, Protestant faith, and connections with England. I have perpetually found myself positioned as an outsider, inevitably becoming a subject of controversy. Similarly,

Germaine, despite your father's esteemed position as a renowned Minister of Finance in France and your sad husband's role as an ambassador representing Sweden in Paris, you were afforded a certain degree of diplomatic protection that I lacked. But you also experienced the status of a foreigner in France.

I feel so nostalgic tonight, remembering Germaine, my best friend and companion in many battles and conflicts. She played a crucial role in helping me embrace my true self, and together we have flourished in the chaotic realms of politics and romance.

I vividly recall that evening, wherein I beheld my beloved Germaine, her countenance pallid and almost as white as her thin hair, in stark contrast to the reddish scarf enveloping her once slender neck, which struggled to support her magnificent head, brimming with ideas and laden with memories of countless battles and love affairs. I knew that day, with a heavy heart, that she would soon succumb before my very eyes. The flickering light of the flames in the dimly lit room only served to intensify the profound sadness of that moment.

I also will die soon, approaching the end of my journey, and I have a strong desire to gather all of my cherished memories into what will likely be my final book. I am immensely grateful to the exceptionally intelligent and talented women who have played a pivotal role in my personal growth, in particular to my beloved Germaine and de Carrier. But I must also express my gratitude to Sieyes and the Count of Clermont-Tonnerre, undoubtedly a wise man, who, like myself, held strong Anglophilic and monarchist beliefs during the tumultuous Assembly of 1787, alongside Mounier and Lally-Tollendal. Unfortunately, they were unable to successfully defend the concept of a democratic monarchy, similar to that of the English, resulting in chaos and the subsequent rise of demagogues like Robespierre,

Danton and finally Napoleon, who ruled and ruined France.

As I sit here in my cold studio, the fire having extinguished several hours ago, I am reminded of the passing of time. The staff must be fast asleep, and at my age, I am no longer capable of tending to the warmth myself. The streets are eerily quiet, and I find myself alone, contemplating what my legacy, if any, will be.

Now that I am old, I am aware that soon I will follow in the steps of Isabelle and Germaine, like many dear friends who left many years ago. I recall the words I pronounced in the cemetery, paying homage to the memory of Germaine, a woman whose mind was truly superior. I try to recall the details of her life, which was characterized, by turns, to winning glory and suffering misfortune.

I know there is little time left, and I still aim to complete at least two works before my mind deteriorates: one on political matters and another on religious subjects. It should be relatively easy to select some text related to my contributions to constitutional law and the significance of human and individual rights.

As a novelist, I take pride in my novella *Adolphe*, which brought me fame not only in France but also in my beloved England, with an almost immediate English translation. My books on history and religion have not yet reached that level of interest, as they have a limited audience. However, some of them have already been translated in Spain and I understand that they have had some influence in Portugal, Brazil, and Mexico, where the struggle to establish a stable and limited government that safeguards citizens' individual rights continues.

Now that I am old, I am aware that soon I will follow in the footsteps of Isabelle and Germaine, like many dear friends who left many years ago. The words I spoke at the cemetery, paying homage to the memory of Germaine left a lasting impression. That sorrowful day was in the midst of a very hot and humid July. I tried then to recall the details of her life, which was dedicated alternately to achieving glory and aiding the unfortunate. Even today, these details present themselves in great numbers and with vividness. When I reread her work, which during her lifetime struck me and her friends for its eloquence, we preferred to dismiss the forebodings that now seem like terrible prophecies of realized events. I wanted to write a eulogy, combining a few words to capture her innumerable qualities. Now, after so many years, a bitter pang seizes me.

Currently, the weather is extremely cold, and it is time for me to retire for the night. As I sit here, I observe the flickering candle, on the verge of extinguishing. Tomorrow, I will embark on the task of writing what I believe will be my final works. In this moment, I find myself unable to escape constant reflections on my past, as well as contemplations on politics, romance, and the adventures of my life.

Without respite, I have dedicated myself to the arduous task of writing, diligently making notes, perusing my extensive collection of books, and reviewing countless letters. My beautiful, dark, and weighty oak desk is now adorned with an assortment of papers, books, and pamphlets. Writing has proven to be a steadfast companion, especially now that the time and energy for pursuing or being pursued by younger or older women has waned. Indeed, thinking and writing remain my loyal companions.

I am deeply grateful for the experiences that have shaped me, particularly the harrowing ordeals of the Napoleonic wars and the terror of the Revolution, which instilled in me a commitment to pacifism and a disdain for autocrats and the masses who support them. While I may not possess a talent for street politics, I relished the opportunity to engage in debates at the Assembly or the Consulate, and even in the intimate setting of an evening Salon. In these discussions, I passionately advocated for a balanced government that safeguards the freedom of religion and the press, while respecting the lives of all individuals, regardless of their social class or wealth.

Anne Marie is a delightful young woman who greets me every morning with a warm smile and a large tray, opening the curtains to reveal the sunny blue sky. Although it appears to be a chilly day, her presence brings warmth to the room. She is both lovely and youthful, communicating with me through polite and responsive words. Despite her petite stature, she effortlessly carries a heavy silver tray filled with coffee, fruit, butter, and bread. I admire her angelic face, framed by casually flowing blonde-golden hair peeking out from under her white linen bonnet. Her eyes are like dark emeralds, a special color that I can not define. As she arranges my pillows and gently adjusts my arms, I can feel the softness of her skin, which contrasts beautifully with her black regimental outfit. Her beauty is captivating, both to behold and to lightly touch. The scent of lavender fills the air, accompanying the flowers that adorn my breakfast platters.

Anne Marie serves as a poignant reminder of what I have lost: my looks, my charms, the desire and the ability to seduce a woman and bring her to my bed. This reality grew slowly, but signs have been with me for some years now. She is from my adored Alsace or Leman, where at one point in my life I was the Consulate Member.

Women have played a significant role in my life. After my time in Scotland and England, I engaged in meaningful relationships with older, married women in Brussels, Paris, and Geneva. Marie-Charlotte Johannot stands out as one of the first women I connected with. Attending social gatherings introduced me to Isabelle de Charrière and Madame de Staël. Isabelle, a respected writer admired by French intellectuals like Diderot, captivated me with her intelligence. Despite our age difference, we shared a mutual charm. Isabelle's husband,

Charles-Emmanuel, a wealthy Swiss, was a close friend of my father. I recall our meeting in Neuchâtel or Paris, not Belgium. I aim to locate our extensive correspondence.

Now I see, I met her in Paris in 1786, three years before the Revolution.

Many think she was the source of inspiration for my *Adolphe*, but she never left her husband or family and even if I was proud with the conquest, I never bragged about it as the character in my novella does. Is true that being so young and having started to learn about different forms of governments and relatively modern ideas during my time in England made me arrogant and conceited. My family from Geneva, particularly, my uncle, openly disliked my character and political ideas. Once, he called me an impertinent young scoundrel, which, now looking at those wild years, was right. My family and close friends have often bailed me out from gambling debts and from what any protestant Swiss would consider unacceptable behavior. After the Revolution started, I no longer took pride in my nights of dissipation and gambling. My life became ruinous, and my physical sufferings brought on by excesses of the night became unbearable.

I know well why older women were so essential in my life, particularly incredibly intelligent and politically active thinkers and writers. No doubt that the greatest cause of the restlessness of my life has been the need for loving. Having so many affairs with older women probably was linked to the fact that I never met my mother, who died very soon after I was born.

My father was wealthy, high ranking official who came from a Swiss Protestant aristocratic family of French Huguenot origin. I grew up with a very severe and cold grandmother and the most diverse types of tutors in different cities and countries. Therefore I did not have a stable home or a stable family. My father was busy and also had many affairs, and married again. I have to thank him for the freedom he gave me and the opportunity to study in a German bording university and then study and have fun in Scotland and England where I learned about the problems facing the corrupt French Royal family and the mismanagement of the country finances. Paradoxically, my beloved Germaine was the daughter of Jacques Necker, Minister of finances of Louis XVI.

As a young, ambitious man, I wonder if my family relations with Swiss Calvinists had any effect upon the attraction I felt for her. I am sure that her status, marrying Baron Erik Magnus Staël, a Swedish diplomat who was 17 years her senior, was a factor. The difference of age was evident, but what really got my attention was her relations with intellectuals and the fact that she already published a book. A copy lies in front of me. Its interesting title is *Lettres sur les ouvrages et le caractère de J.J. Rousseau*. Roussea is a thinker with whom I had fundamental differences.

I can say now that I became entirely captivated by her personality, intellect, conversation, and particularly her moderate ideas at a troubled and dangerous time. She had royalist leanings but welcomed the constitutionalist cause, starting with her support of the meetings of the Estates-General. She was also clear on her open sympathy for individual freedoms that were constantly assaulted during the disastrous first five years of the Revolution.

She played a crucial role in my involvement in political life during the emergence of a new regime. The influence of Germaine and the connections I established at her Paris salon proved to be invaluable, leading me to The Directory. I identified myself as a moderate royalist and harbored high expectations for the new regime in France. My support for The Directory stemmed from my desire to preserve and enhance the positive outcomes of the Revolution, while also aiming to prevent a resurgence of the Jacobins' Terror or the bankrupt monarchy of the Ancien Régime. She demonstrated foresight by recognizing the rise of Napoleon from the outset and engaging in a struggle with him. Napoleon subjected her to surveillance before ultimately prohibiting her from residing near Paris. I joined her, and together we embarked on an idyllic exile, initially in Germany and later at her castle in Coppet.

There have been quite a few coincidences. Isabelle de Charrière also wrote two books on Rousseau, one of whose most ardent critics I have been and still am, especially regarding Rousseau's ideas on freedom and tyranny. Isabelle first published "Confessions de Rousseau" and a few years later a title that still makes me angry today, "Eloge de Jean-Jacques Rousseau" ("Praise for . . ."). I delivered a speech that compared our perspectives on the concept of freedom between the ancients and the moderns. I lean towards individual freedom and a government with limited powers. Rousseau, on the other hand, followed the ancient notion of a Greek democracy where the individual must be subject to an assembly. As demonstrated in France over the last thirty years, such bodies can enable various forms of despotism. After my daily walk, I will check my library for my essay and celebrated speech on the topic of old and modern concepts of freedom.

I've had numerous debates about this issue with individuals who may not share the same perspective. It's hard to overlook the events during the Revolutionary Terror and the subsequent rise of Napoleon's supporters, leading to widespread suffering and oppressive governance that sparked the concept of collective self-determination. It's a challenge to establish a citizen's identity closely linked to the community as a whole. I've often questioned Rousseau's followers about which specific community they refer to, considering the diverse range of communities, some of which endorse autocratic regimes or advocate for restrictions on freedom of the press, religion, and speech. Our recent history provides several instances of such communities.

It is good to go for a walk. I was getting angry arguing with Rousseau and the demagogues, who use his old ideas and the notion of collective rule. It is cold but the sky is so blue, no clouds or wind making unpleasant my look at the historic garden. So much history here before and after the Revolution. The Tuileries is an old garden designed almost three hundred years ago as an Italian garden. It hosted kings, magnificent parties and concerts were played in the now destroyed pavilions. They were destroyed mostly by the angry and destructive crowds that stormed the Louvre Palace. Is difficult to imagine the violence and the battles happening here. Now, everything is quiet and it is a treat to be walking on the terraces, contemplating the naked trees. Even the lack of flowers makes the royal buildings that surround it more grand. I wonder how many designers and famous architects transformed the space. I enjoy walking in the light brown siena sand, the wide paths and the now empty islands for plants without the color of the spring flowers. Now, they have only dry shrubs. Few people are walking at this time, some elegant women with their kids. Yes there are some men but my eyes are always distracted by my opposite sex.

We are still living in a turbulent time, but fortunately far from the time when Robespierre not far from here set fire to the mannequins that represented Atheism, Ambition, Selfishness, Discord, and False Simplicity, revealing a statue of Wisdom, surrounded by crowd that I am sure screamed and wildly applauded him. Interesting that I am waking near the fountain where the coffin of

Jean-Jacques Rousseau lay in those dark days, and from here his bones were taken to the Pantheon.

The weather is nice on my walk under the sun, making the cold more tolerable. I have the energy to try to cross the Seine and go to the Assemblée Nationale. It is so peaceful to see so many women washing cloth in the river and loudly talking. I wonder how they live, what kind of families and homes they have. It should not be far. The group of five or seven are modestly dressed and seem to be happy with what they are doing. They are bended, crouching out, with the skirts to their knees, showing their naked legs. The older is plump and round, while the younger one is skinny and slender. If I were a painter, I would use this bucolic scene with the river, its bridges, some boats slowly sliding in the tranquil waters reflecting the sky. I can also see Notre-Dame. So many colors and forms. That is why I love Paris and call it mine after so many turns.

I am standing in front of the Assemblée Nationale, remembering that it hosted The Directory and became a meeting place of the different post-revolution assemblies that moved from the old, empty royal theater of the Tuileries. Originally it was the Palais Bourbon, but suffered so many changes during different governments. At the time of Napoleon's French Empire, the façade changed to mirror that of the Church of the Madeleine. If I turn around, I can see the twin building across the Seine and the Place de la Concorde, the square where cheering crowds met to look at public executions, including those of King Louis XVI, Marie Antoinette and at the end, paradoxically, Robespierre. With him, the cruelest time of the French Revolution started to become washed out and have dramatic turns. It makes me dizzy thinking of the carousel I have lived.

From where I am standing now, looking at the washing ladies in the Seine, I can see the Louvre Palace and most of the spaces that served as stage for the tragic history of France during the Revolution.

I don't think I am far from the home of the Countess de Linières, where I met so many people when I arrive in Paris from England, arrogant and bankrupt from gambling and dissipation. The parties in that house increased my already-terrible reputation. That is why when my father learned of my adventures he decided it was time to find me a suitable wife who would check my excesses (and especially help to pay my gambling debts). My father was not the only one busily trying to pick a suitable woman for me; the old ladies in my father's social world were involved as well. I remember the ultimatum my father presented to me: he with all his authority and seriousness told me to find a lady or quit Paris to live with him in the Bois-le-Duc, a terrible choice.

Since no wife was found, my father send to Germany to the Court of the Duke of Brunswick where I was assigned a boring ceremonial post of Gentleman of the Under-chamberlain. Those years filled me with tedium and frustration, especially remembering Paris and England where I had been free. I was not idle; I dedicated time to the history of the of the Greek civilization and traditions that led Greece up to the destruction of Troy. I also start comparing the customs of the Greeks with the customs of the Celts, Germans, Scots, Scandinavians, and other cultures. It was one year before the French Revolution started. Even if I tried hard then and pledged to never to play at any game of chance, I failed and would receive a reprimand from my Grandmother and my beloved Isabelle.

It was then I made the terrible choice to marry to a lady-in-waiting at the court. Her name was Luise Johanne von Cram, or Mina as I used to call her. She was eight years older than me. My father was horrified and opposed the marriage not only for the age difference, but for her lack of fortune. I knew very soon she was not for me, we were so different in taste and lifestyle. To make it worse, the court atmosphere was made for cheating, and both of us had affairs. Mina very openly dated a Russian prince. We constantly fought, and divorce was unavoidable. With her dissipated conduct and distant demeanor, we lacked any basic communication. That mix of negative circumstances made it easy for me to have Mina sign the separations papers when I requested her to.

With a broken hart I decided to return to Switzerland in August 1794, and it was there that my my guardian angel led me to meet my two saviors and pillars of my productive life, full, intense romance, and political struggle. Germaine de Staël was the most important relationship, a life full of twists until she died. Before that providential meeting, I lived though a depressive, nostalgic, and sad period of loneliness that felt like a shipwreck. Luckily, Mme.de Charriérre became a peaceful port mainly when she invited me to move to her Château Colombier near Neuchâtel for four months. It was a difficult time with the Swiss in panic of emigration. In those early days of the Revolution in France, hundreds of nobles and priests from France escaping the terror and nationalization of their assets and homes, arrived in Switzerland, some optimistic, fantasizing they would soon return to France and restore the old regime. My host, as always, was busy writing and hosting dozens of French refugees in Neuchâtel. It was at that time when her book, *Lettres trouvées dans des porte-feuilles d'émigrés* was published.

The interaction with Isabelle after studying in England and serving in a German Court, made me more focused and interested in politics. I was 23 years old and surrounded with all sorts of people—some, attacking a certain type of aristocracy, for being lazy, corrupt and arrogant—others committed to recovering what they had lost and ready to support a new king. At that time, Louis XVI was guillotined, the Convention instituted the Public Health Committee which consolidated in France the path to Terror with the Guillotine in full swing and the constant looting of the sans-culottes, making Paris the most dangerous place on earth.

My love for adventures guided me to seriously think about the social and political future of France, especially listening to the guests of Isabelle, a remarkable woman who was an active advocate for the equality of men and women and the right to freedom. To be associated with Madame de Charrière, a brilliant writer in the quietude of her countryside home in such turbulent times, allowed me to witness the debates with the ideas of freedom and stable government. This experience was decisive and I became what was called then a moderate Republican. I started to denounce censorship and the violence in the name of the people. I openly advocated for a United Kingdom type of parliament with two governing bodies or assemblies. It was then when I started to think of ways to directly participate in the government, which I accomplished five years later as a member of the Tribunal representing Léman region when the Republic of Geneva was annexed to the French Republic. The terror was over, but dissent was not allowed and that was why I only served there for a few years.

The contrast of those stories we heard from immigrants who arrived bankrupt from France in 1793 with the easy life in Colomber, with its easy informal conversations, walking in the carefully designed French garden and the orchard with trees with cherries and apples, was extraordinary. I remember sitting in a bench inside a Chinese gazebo right next to a little brook, looking at the lake surrounded with small villages and vineyards full of red and white grapes shining in the sun, ready to be collected. But there also were the horror stories of hell from Paris described by the immigrants in the context of this true paradise. At my age, this paradise became every day more monotonous and boring, and I was prepared to act.

I feel tired from walking now, and have a headache from thinking so much. When the age of passions has passed, what can we want except to escape from life with as little pain as possible? But memories, both good and bad, are bubbling up. Today it was impossible to avoid going back in time, as I decided to take a stroll past the theater venues where the Revolution had been staged. The garden of the Tuileries, the National Assembly, and the Place de la Concorde have hosted various dreadful events that occurred nearly forty years ago.

The dinner that Anne Marie prepared was wonderful, I always like duck breast and with cherry sauce and probably some honey to make it perfect. The claret Anne Marie brought to accompany the food paired well.

I had a lovely evening strolling in Paris, reminiscing about my time at Château Colombiere with Mdm. de Charrière. However, it was Germaine, my companion in numerous personal and political adventures, who truly captured my heart. Encountering Mme. de Staël in Nyon felt like a miracle after life at Mme. de Charrière's Château Colombier became monotonous and dull, leading to increasing tension and making my life quite miserable.

I had decided to leave, and after some days, I remember riding fast when a carriage with an interesting woman waving passed. It then stopped. I turned and went back, and then, everything started. First, it was an easy and friendly conversation since we both knew of each other by rumors and gossip. I knew she hosted interesting Salons in Paris; she knew my family and my dissipated life was a bit like hers. After some time exchanging pleasantries, she invited me to ride in her carriage to continue the conversation, recognizing a common interest in politics and social life. She was aware that I recently had been a guest of Isabella, and since I was very outspoken, she found me amusing. I assume that from that moment, we both knew that we had found the best companion and confidant for the rest of our lives.

During the fortuitous trip in her carriage, she extended an invitation for me to stay at Coppet, her castle near Geneva. I needed a new mentor, and life had brought me one, but I never imagined what that relationship would represent.

Germaine wanted to go back to Paris and again start a Salon with the idea of reconciling the moderates of the right and those of the left so that France could obtain the peace it deserved. I found myself with someone who helped me to convert into a liberal, and discovered the main ambition of my life, to be a writer and to become an ardent defender of individual freedom and to call attention of the dangers of crowds and populism to the individual.

I saw in Germaine something more than a new mentor and a home maker. At that time, I was already thirty years old or more but I never had until then had a stable home—my father moved constantly, and living for short periods with my grandmother never felt like a home. Germaine made me feel that her castle in Coppet was my residency.

The rest of my family knew the Neckers well since our two families lived around Lake Geneva, but I had not known them until the fortunate encounter with Germaine and my first visit to Coppet.

I have fresh in my memory arriving with her in the carriage to the wonderful avenue of willows that leads to the castle. It was already late but in that golden hour the lake was shining with the colors of a glorious sunset. I was beyond excited to meet my future. I loved the garden which at night had the aromas of herbs and spices. The old castle is shaded by gigantic chestnut trees and is surrounded by a thick forest of very tall trees. It lacks views of the lake which is very near. The village is lovely with old fountains and a dark stone church. It was a charming spot with very special surroundings that hosted me for years. This was there where my beloved Germaine lived her last years until she died in the idyllic place. I hope I will be that lucky.

My relation with her was not truly romantic; we hardly became lovers since she was always surrounded by suitors and generally held short term but intense romances. Our relationship was mostly of an intellectual nature, with common personal interests which forged a close political collaboration. This became evident when I wrote the note dated in Paris in 1797 that I am holding in my hand. I want to read this in a loud voice, since I am alone and at peace in my studio:

"We promise to consecrate our lives to each other; we declare that we feel inextricably united with each other, that we will always share the same destiny, that we will never bond with any other person, and that we will strengthen the bond that already unites us as soon as we are given to do so.

I declare that I accept this promise with all the sincerity of my heart, that I do not know anything on earth that is more valuable to me than the love of Mme. de Staël, that throughout the four months that I have spent by her side I have been the happiest man in the world and that I consider the greatest of things to be able to make her happy in her youth, to age quietly by her side and reach the end next to the soul that understands me and without whose presence life on earth would cease to interest me."

Looking at this document, now a bit crumpled and definitively old, I recognize that the author was her. We were in her studio and she brought some paper and ink and start dictating. Naturally, I agreed with the idea since many times we discussed her intentions which by then were mine. It was not a formal marriage, since she was still married. Notwithstanding the romantic nature of our promise, we did not keep it. Soon, we both continued to have romantic adventures and a plethora of love affaires.

I owe her so much. I feel so tired now and nostalgic for a life full of glorious moments and a great deal of pain. My studio is full of so many other papers and letters that we exchanged during her life, as well as dozens from my Isabelle, my early mentor who was also of great importance in my oscillated life full of turns.

These two women, with all the twists and conflicts we had, are surely the most important characters in my life. I am happy to go to my bed, covered with a heavy red wool or muslin cover. I see that my big chest next to me is full of books and papers, a reminder to keep writing. I have such a disorder and not a long time left to decide what will probably be the last project I pursue with full mental awareness.

I blow out the smoking oil lamp after looking at the image of Saint Paul, a large painting probably a present from Germaine. None of us held religious faith, even if she, like Paul, in her last moments, converted to Catholicism to get the sacred oils from a local priest.

Every night I go to bed with the pleasure of reflecting on what the next day will bring, knowing that there are few days left. I recall the greatest pleasures, deceptions, and betrayals along with the most drastic political changes. I was an active political figure, serving as a controversial speaker, writer, and member of various governments, always advocating for equality and freedom. Unfortunately, despite all the bloodshed since 1789, the ideals of freedom, equality, and fraternity are far from being realized.

A lovely morning, again. I open my eyes with pleasure to look at Anne Marie's smile as she brings the coffee and opens the heavy green curtains. The day is bright again, but is cold. I should stay home. My desk full of papers and books waits for me.

Tomorrow, Charlotte will be back after a long visit to her family in Germany. With her at home, a busy daily life will resume. She likes to receive visitors, so our home will be noisy with late-night dinners and musical soirées. I am at stage of life where big groups make me tired. Conversations on trivial gossip bore me. That's why I am glad that I have to visit my constituency soon, giving her space to entertain her friends. I have to admit that I enjoyed the solitude as a rich and busy bachelor, but aging alone is not secure. I feel sorry for these thoughts, proving that even at this age I continue to be selfish and a bit of a cynic.

I cannot complain after so many years of marriage. Charlotte has been a good companion and always shows care for me. I especially appreciate it now that my health has been deteriorating; my legs are weak and I need her support.

Like me, she has been married two times before, and marrying me in secret was a controversial move for both of us. She comes from a noble German family. Her father, Hans Ernst von Hardenberg, has been a treasurer and advised the Hanover delegation in London where Charlotte was born.

We met in the Court of the Duke of Brunswick while I was there. When I saw her for the first time, I found her not only a beautiful woman but also, for a change, a woman who was only two years older than me. Her conversation was witty and easy to like. We flirted, but there were big impediments to making our relationship serious. I was married to Mina, and she was also married. We fell in love, and she was willing to divorce her first husband to marry me, but I did not dare, even though I was having so many troubles with Mina and finding marriage dull and complicated.

I still keep a box containing romantic letters I composed for Charlotte, replete with risqué advances and obvious intentions. During that period, nothing substantial transpired, only pleasant, discreet moments that we shared, but my standing in the Court had deteriorated. The Duke had openly expressed his disgust with my still immature and wild behavior, which did not align well with his Court.

To escape from the Court, a new marriage was not the solution. The best course of action I found was to accept Mme. de Charrière's invitation to once again become a guest at her Chateau in Neuchâtel. Leaving the Court completely changed my life. I was finally able to divorce Mina and start anew, but it took years before I encountered Charlotte again, this time in Paris. I saw her at a formal dinner with her husband. She was now known as Mme. du Tertre. She had married a French officer with a noble title in Hanover. It was evident that her marriage was not a happy one. On that fateful night, she took the initiative, showing a renewed interest in me. During that social dinner, her smiles and demeanor were so unmistakable that they made her husband uncomfortable and visibly jealous. We rekindled our flirtation and correspondence, discreetly avoiding public acknowledgment of our relationship. After a few weeks, she left Paris without a clear direction for our relationship. I was keen to establish a bond, and she seemed receptive to my advances and willing to consider a change. It was around eighteen months later that we met again, and it became apparent that I had also fallen in love with her. She captivated me with her charm, wit, kindness, and gentleness, qualities that still bring me immense happiness to this day. Our intimacy developed swiftly, convincing me that a formal union with her would bring tranquility into my life. She agreed to end her marriage, and finally, Charlotte became my lawful wife.

Learning through gossip about my marriage with Charlotte was a source of great sorrow for my esteemed friend, Madame de Staël, as reported by mutual acquaintances. Her entire demeanor regarding this matter revealed her fickle and unreliable nature on romantic issues, as following the passing of Baron de Staël, she declined my proposals for several years. Upon hearing news of my impending marriage, she confided in a mutual acquaintance that she could not bear the thought of my marrying another.

Like the revolutions and political movements in France, the character of my beloved Germaine could easily change and become violent and intolerant. I reflect on her positive influence on my life, our fortuitous encounter on the route to Coppet that saved me from suicide, and how she transformed my life by welcoming me into her circle, providing me with a place to live, conspiring together against Napoleon, and nurturing me in various ways. I also recall her negative bitterness and extreme anger when my happy marriage was revealed and became known to her.

To complicate that cherished relationship, one year before my wedding, gossip started to circulate about a recently born daughter of Mme. de Staël named Albertine whose features, hair, everything, in fact, appeared to be a striking likenesses of me. The public, without any evidence, saw the resemblance as equivocal proof of my paternity, which I emphatically denied. It served my enemies to paint me as a calculating soul with many liaisons of love and friendship, including a distant and cold relationship with Albertine, my natural daughter as assigned by the public. Today, after so many years and with Albertine married, her mother and legal father are dead; living an independent life has allowed us to avoid trying to solve the mystery of her paternity. We mainly know that Germaine had multiple affairs during the time she was conceived.

These events provided me with an excuse to escape again from Coppet and bury myself in some form of hermitage. I had the opportunity for solitary reflection on my long and peculiar state of dependence upon Germaine. I refused to be any longer the satellite of a brilliant meteor. Marriage to another woman had seemed the only means of escape, and fortunately a miracle happened with the encounter with my Charlotte, in those days Mme. du Tertre.

After all the drama, my relationship with Germaine and the Coppet group, which had played such a significant role in my life for nearly seventeen years, continued with the usual ups and downs until the day she passed away. I recall that Albertine's husband, the Duc de Broglie, and I kept vigil together for one night beside Mme. de Staël as she was fading and dying. In the last few days, I have continued to think back on that sad night, marked by particular grief and some remorse probably for not having fully expressed my appreciation for all she had done for me.

There exist numerous concealed and undoubtedly many incongruous recollections of my tumultuous life. I cannot attribute Charlotte's return this evening to those melancholic moments that persist in haunting me at this advanced age. Charlotte was an acquaintance of Germaine's, perceived as a rival to her position in my life. Their casual friendship endured, despite a growing distance that widened after the marriage. Both are well-educated individuals who maintained decorum when in each other's company, especially in public settings.

I need to stop these thoughts to focus and decide what to write and start working. Time is running out, I'm aware. I'm considering topics like religion, politics, or other memories. The last option seems easiest because lately I've been dwelling on past experiences, people I've met, and events I've witnessed or been a part of. Germaine was right when she said, "As we grow older, we find ourselves living in the past, as there is little future left." I have to handle memories carefully, as there are uncomfortable truths about my character. Those who think my novella *Adolphe* is autobiographical are partly correct. It's not a complete self-portrait or a direct description of Mme. de Charrière or Germaine, one of the women who dominated me. The situations with both were similar to my Novella; older women, married, friends of my youth, dissatisfied and lonely, their minds their only resource, and both fond of analyzing everything with wit. I wrote *Adolphe* with a sense of self-pity and a desire to escape a condition, reflecting on the strong bond that had developed between Madame de Staël and me, which had become like a chain of iron.

Reflecting on memoirs, I also need to consider what I have written in my *Cahier Rouge*, which I had composed before *Adolphe* and which remains unpublished, but it is widely read in various formats, mostly distributed by acquaintances and adversaries. In that text, I primarily focused on my childhood, education, and the succession of tutors and monks hired by my father, after my mother passed away a few days after my birth. It was not an easy childhood, I must admit. The narrative includes numerous biographical elements, particularly my studies at the University of Edinburgh, where I encountered the British philosopher and politicians James Mackintosh and Malcolm Laing. I also recounted my early journeys to Paris, detailing the inception of my significant relationship with Isabelle de Charrière, my savior and host during those challenging times. Additionally, I discussed my family, including my strict grandmother and beloved Aunt Pauline, who played pivotal roles in my life, especially during my extravagant years in Paris and also at the very dark times at the German Court.

There were other brief yet intense romantic encounters with older women, apart from Germaine and Isabelle. One such instance involved an English woman named Mrs. Trevor, who lived in Switzerland, who was married and older, also resembling the character in *Adolphe*. Mrs. Trevor possessed a very coquettish demeanor, charming expressions, and a delightful smile. As was the case with all romances during that period, I swiftly fell in love with her.

Some individuals consider my *Cahier* to have a similar style to Rousseau's *Confessions*, which is a good reason not to write another biography. My last book has to be serious, therefore a memoire will imply looking at the hundreds of letters I have written and received at different times to my family, my lovers, my wives, my mentors, protegés, political colleagues, and also my enemies. This is a task I am not currently in a position to handle seriously due to the time it would take and the self-censorship it would require in selecting different moments and people.

Loving women as I did, always terrorized me, specially to inflicting pain, since I can easily suffer by feminine tears. It was depressive to becoming restive under their tyranny and never easy to break a relationship and to leave. That is the theme of *Adolphe*, the burden the character describes in his "*Journal Intime*." I cannot deny that those feelings mimic mine at that time to free myself from Mme. de Staël. My life was burdened by a destructive dependance and by indecision since I was unable to give up anything!

My *Adolphe* took me many years to complete. It was the subject of many revisions. Before I even start writing it, dramatic changes were happening in France. After six years, the bloody era of the Revolution faded with the end of the reign of Terror, and the Assembly was replaced by the Directory, which restored some sense of normal life to France in 1795. That good news led Germaine and I to leave the glorious days in Coppet, and we got back to Paris to the Swedish Embassy in Rue de Bac. The Baron of Staël had presented again his credentials as ambassador of Sweden, this time to the new French Republic. The Ambassador welcomed us back and accepted me as their guest, even though rumors made me the lover of his wife, which were partially true. When we arrived, we were terrified to look at the ruins of revolution. The convents and abbeys were abandoned; Notre-Dame was a storehouse for wine casks, the Bonnet-rouge decorated the public buildings, and the palaces of the scattered nobles were used as storehouses, cafés and auction rooms, where all sorts of plunder was exposed for sale: carved and inlaid furniture from looted mansions, mirrors, ornaments, paintings and statues taken from the altars of the saints. The Palais Royal, formerly the resort of the aristocracy, had a new name: the Palais Egalité.

Paris, the beautiful city we left years before, was difficult to recognize. There was runaway inflation making people hungry and ready to revolt again. There was a new class of rich *citoyen* who made their fortunes with the nationalized assets of foreigners. The new Republic auctioned churches at ridiculous prices, anticipating the struggle of an exhausted Paris to continue. For me as a defender of individual freedom who distrusts mob movements, the sight of Paris post-revolution, reaffirmed my convictions regarding revolutions as a source of corruption: they provide enormous economic benefits to their leaders on top of their new political power.

As was expected, a new popular insurrection broke out. This time Barras, the head of the Directory, appointed Napoleon Bonaparte (the future emperor and soon our political enemy) to use the army to crush the rebellion of the royalists, an action that led to the killing of thousands of unarmed men and women. That horrific act made Napoleon a "hero" who, according to his followers, saved the Republic.

After our arrival in Paris, Germaine was not well received by those in power. Rumors had started to circulate, implicating her and, by association, me in conspiracies against the Directory in light of the upcoming elections. I made serious errors in my writings for *Les Nouvelles Politiques* regarding the proposed numbers from different factions and the procedure for electing members of a new Legislative Convention. Initially, I vehemently opposed the election's decree; however, later I extended my support towards it. Reflecting on that period, I now realize how youthful, arrogant, and inexperienced I was, validating Germaine's view of me as too immature to engage in politics.

The Swedish Embassy in Paris became known as the New Rue de Bac Salon, becoming again as animated and controversial as it had been during the first years of the Revolution. Talleyrand (later Napoleon's Minister of Foreign Relations) and Comte de Narbonne (Germaine's former lover and the father of her son) were regular guests. These men and other participants in the Salon, at that time of the young Revolution, were considered enemies. After the Terror was defeated, they started to become rehabilitated and gained new political power and recognition.

Together with the activities in the newly reopened Salon, Germaine's writings caused her to be considered again a dangerous enemy, therefore she was soon ordered to leave Paris. For my part, as her political associate, I was attacked for my writings and unfairly accused of being a foreigner, which by residence and law I was not. These circumstances gave me no other choice but to leave Paris with her. Facing serious threats, we decided to go back again to Coppet to find a safe refuge and start a new period of our lives, one that would turn out to be highly intellectually productive.

Coppet became a real writing workshop where we produced many books and pamphlets, some of which are now piled on the desk in front of me. I don't remember when many of the titles were published, only the most celebrated. The working atmosphere was so intense that even M. Necker, inspired by his daughter's passion for writing, wrote about the state of finances in France, a subject that he dominated as a former Minister of Finance. The title of his book that should be someplace in my bookcase is *Dernières Vues de Politique et de Finance*. The book was doomed to fail because of its timing and the connections of the author, particularly since Napoleon openly disliked Germaine. The treaty on politics and finance that Necker had written with the intention of making it his legacy to posterity ended up infuriating the First Consul.

Germaine dedicated herself to completing her *Treatise on passions*, with the title *De l'influence des passions sur le bonheur des individus et des nations*, published in 1796, shortly after we moved back from Paris to Coppet, by Jean Mourer et Hignou, a Lausanne publisher. This book was followed years later by two novels: *Delphine* a controversial book that made her famous for her description of the conditions of women in France (and her ardent defense of women), followed by *Corinne*. I have to admit with some caveats that it is possible to see Germaine's novellas as "inverted mirrors" of *Adolphe*, since the victim is not a tormented married woman who falls madly in love with a younger and selfish lover, but a married man who falls in love with a woman who makes him suffer as she does with other men. I, like Mme de Staël, also used the main characters' names as the titles.

During that time in Coppet, there were heated discussions among us about her writings, especially the *Passions*. That book has been well received because of its chapters on various emotions and traits that appeal to many readers, building on Germaine's well-deserved fame as a writer with a deep understanding of the human condition. The book features captivating chapter titles such as "Love," "Fame," "Virtue," "Envy," and "Revenge," which resonate with a wide audience. Given Germaine's political interests, it was expected that she would add the political element; another type of passion, *Party Loyalty* (*De l'esprit de parti*), describing the darker aspects of partisan politics where fanaticism and intolerance are wisely depicted: "Throughout the centuries marred by religious disputes, we witnessed individuals of somber countenance, resorting to every conceivable method and braving all perils in their unwavering dedication to the cause they had embraced." Germaine cited the Revolution and the outcome in France in 1795, making this "passion" easy to recognize, especially when she referred to the divisions at the Constituent Assembly, where the members on the right side could have passed some of the decrees that interested them, if they would have compromised and listened to the moderate side. "A triumph achieved by condescension was a defeat for their party," she wrote, adding, "the integrity of dogma is even more important than the success of the cause." I vividly remember our conversation about this topic;

we denounced the dogmatic attitude of members of the new and old political classes.

Now, after more than thirty years, seated comfortably in my studio, opening her red leather-bound book (which is worn since I regularly read it), it is clear to me that one of the passions or characters she described is related to or inspired by me. I remember how many times we discussed the makeup of human traits, which led us to our usual fights. In one instance, reading one of the drafts, I feel insulted when she maked it clear it was my dissipated past life and selfish character that were the key to writing the section titled "Gambling, Avarice, Drunkenness, etc." We remained silent for a moment as she started again to argue in her rough authoritarian voice, which made me rise from my chair and abruptly walk towards the door. Before I left, I vividly remember her mocking voice telling me not to try to commit suicide again, a reference to my past tantrums. I became visibly angry, leaving the room determined to pack and leave, using her unpleasant attitude as the perfect excuse.

Our relationship became tense in the days that followed these unpleasant incidents, and as I can see from the letters I wrote and am holding now, it was in March 1796 when the contacts I made with Abbé Sieyès, a prominent member of the Directory, helped me to return to Paris for what I thought would be a respite from romantic agitations and the beginning of a long path to politics. It took me some days to prepare and decide not to share my plans with Germaine. She was angry and unfriendly all the time, probably because she knew I was ready to leave Coppet and venture into politics. The fight about her book on *Passions* anticipated my move, making her more offensive to me. I did not contest the veracity of her assertion that self-doubt is a persistent facet of my character. The challenge of making the decision to depart from Coppet and Germaine, fully cognizant of the lasting consequences it would bring about, provided a stark illustration of this characteristic.

A few hours after this vexatious incident, I remember how she entered the dining room for the evening meal. As always, she was seated at the head of the table, stern, to show she was in control. During dinner, we kept silent, allowing it to pass off without incident. The next day, relative peace returned after I once more accepted her balanced mixture of authority and generosity. I was aware that Germaine used me as a model to write about those passions, but also, a few years after this event, she accepted that in her two novels, one of the characters' personalities was inspired by me. Today, I don't know if I should take it as a compliment. One of her novel-writing talents was to realistically replicate people, conversations, and situations familiar to her. In the case of *Delphine*, she used me as a model and also included her own experiences to idealize who she would have liked to be.

Another memory of Germaine from the time when she was writing her *Passions*, the book that I am holding now, is of her in Copper's library picking up reference books from Greek and Roman classics to get inspiration and examples. She also used Jean Racine's *Phèdre* as an example of what is to be under the yoke of fatality, the same with the lyric poet Anacreon. I also remember her seated at a table, close to a window in the luxurious Necker library, attentively looking at religious Fifteenth or Sixteenth Century Italian paintings in a book, referring to those images as producing music or poetry with "madrigalic spirit" a term she coined at that moment. She told me that by interpreting those images as voluptuous made her relate them to Ovid's verses of "Dido," "Ceyx," and "Alcyone" from *Metamorphoses*.

The library was a uniquely attractive working place for both of us with high ceilings and full of leather bound books. It was easy to search for authors, subjects or eras, since their library was organized by a professional English librarian. Right next to the main room, in an open space was a small study, the walls of which were lined with a satin fabric of soft red or green. I cannot recall precisely how they looked, but I am certain that the floor was covered with colorful Persian carpets. The furniture included a tall, simple, handsome revolving oak bookcase to hold the books we used for reference or research. It was conveniently close to a long writing table that both of us could use at the same time. I recall a few Italian bronze statuettes, and a tall green heating stove in a corner.

The library with its heavy, dark wooden shelves filled from floor to ceiling with white, red and different hues of brown leather binding was where we passed our days finishing our projects; Germaine worked on her *Passions* and I was finishing a long essay on government. I was organizing my ideas to avoid costly mistakes. From the title, I made it clear in the most explicit terms that it was my desire to serve, considering it a duty to join the government and actively participate in a struggle for individual freedom. *De la force du gouvernement actuel de la France et de la nécessité de s'y rallier* (On the strength of France's current government and the need to rally to it) was published in the *Moniteur* as a serial, followed by a printing as an individual pamphlet. It served its purpose and opened the door to get me back to Paris to start a serious political life in the Directory, and later in the Tribunant. Many of the ideas in that early work serve as a basis for *Principles of Politics Applicable to All Governments*, another book I wrote fifteen years later in Paris.

I owe my appointment to the Tribunat in some measure to Germaine, who many years before had introduced me to Barras, one of my sponsors. But it was the Abbé Sieyès (Emmanuel Joseph), who read my pamphlet and convince Napoleon Bonaparte to designate me. Unfortunately my close connection with Mme de Staël, together with the radical content of my speeches, made the Consul force me into exile, closing a short chapter in the long political path that follows through today. Before I was forced to resign, as a preview, I had the bitter experience of seeing my name receive the most bitter attacks from my enemies in both camps. The *Feuille du Jour*, a widely read journal of the time, once again called me a foreigner, asking why I did not comply with the law requiring all foreigners to leave Paris. It was an early warning, and prepared me to leave Paris again to ask refuge at Coppet. Being called a foreigner made me lose my mind and I immediately demanded reparation from the editor and the author for their unfair attacks, which led us to the Bois de Boulogne for a duel, which, following my aversion to violence, ended in reconciliation.

I do not think it is a good idea to revisit the past, especially now that my wife Charlotte is returning. I must acknowledge Germaine for the numerous actions that have supported me and helped me grow. I particularly admired her consistent stance of being against the current, in opposition, regardless of the situation. At the beginning she was for the Coup of 18 Fructidor, when some members of the Directorate led by Sieyès and Paul Barras seized control, with the expulsion more than fifty directors, in some cases with jail or exile. Germaine, with some reason, considered them victims. That event marked the beginning of the end for the Directorate, and created more tension between us. She called me an opportunist when I congratulated the Directors for their measures and avoided committing to the victims of the Coup. Today, looking back, having experienced what followed, I am aware that she was right to consider that coup d'État as the first step to despotism. Even if she seriously tried to see Napoleon as an option to promote our ideas of progressive political rights in a free society, in the end, she saw him as the worst of the tyrants. After the second Coup of 18 Brumario, which elevated Bonaparte to First Consul of the Republic, France had taken an initial step on the path that would lead him to have absolute power.

It is late and Charlotte should arrive soon. It has been a day of recollecting very personal moments mostly linked with my intellectual and political life so closely connected to Germaine, but also a day of recollecting the financial stability that I enjoy. I cannot deny that I started accumulating wealth beyond my family's small inheritance with the support of Germaine's father, Jacques Necker, who was the former Finance Minister for Louis XVI. He loaned me the money to buy and fix a half-abbey in ruins in Hérivaux, near Paris, offered by the French Government selling confiscated assets. Germaine and I believe I remember her father have stayed there with me after Napoleon invaded Geneva, making them and me unquestionable French citizens.

I'm feeling tired now and I believe that writing another memoir or biography will be challenging and controversial, especially after a day filled with memories, some of which are vague in terms of moments and names. Especially as I reflect today, it's hard to deny that Germaine continues to have a significant influence on my life, even though it is many years since her passing.

I had a good conversation with Charlotte during dinner. She returned full of life, her skin shining and a bit tan since she had been visiting friends in Palermo, breaking with the bitter cold of Hanover's winter. She was elegantly dressed as if attending a formal dinner, and compelled me to dress for the occasion, marking a change from the months I have dined alone. Our cook prepared her favorite "Magrets de canard aux cerises" that we accompanied with a rouge Malbec de Chaos, one of my preferred wines. I was happy to learn that all her family are doing well and it seems she had a great time, even though she insisted on telling me how much she missed me.

At this point in our marriage, romance and intimacy have logically faded. We have managed to maintain our friendship, relative loyalty, and companionship. We share similar interests and Charlotte has been a great support for my political activities. She mentioned and brought with her the last novel by Victor Hugo, *Le Dernier Jour d'un Condamné* (The Last Day of a Condemned Man). Like the title suggests, it narrates the horrific story of a family and a man condemned to death at the guillotine, following the example of the many killed the same way during the Terror period of the Revolution. I share Victor Hugo's views, not only on the issue of the death penalty but also on the idea of public executions, which bring out the worst of the human condition, when looks at a mob, a shouting crowd insulting at the man or woman who will die in such a horrific way.

I assume she is now sleeping after her long trip. It has been a long time since we shared a bed, even for some moments of intimate contact. I feel old, weak, and no longer attractive. I appreciate her understanding during the times I was distracted and distressed thinking of Germaine and Albertine, with a heart full of regrets. Charlotte's gentleness helped me avoid continual recollection during the early years of our marriage while Germaine was still alive. Breaking away from them was difficult, knowing the pain and damage it caused Germaine before she passed away. I am grateful to my wife for her support and understanding, helping me through those dark days.

I am ready to fall asleep, trying to stop thinking. I want to wake up tomorrow with a clear mind and finally decide what should be the last work I write. I know she cannot hear me since she should be by now sleeping in the room next door. I want to say it in a loud voice, "Good night and thank you, my sweet Charlotte, for all that you have done."

Every day, Anne Marie brings me breakfast and opens the heavy curtains. It's a daily ritual of warmth from someone who has faithfully served us for many years. Adding to this morning delight is the aroma of freshly brewed coffee. From my bed, I see a cloudy, dark day, feeling the chill in the air, possibly hinting at a late March snow, a rarity. Charlotte is likely sleeping next door after her trip.

Returning to our routine, we will have lunch together. There is a welcome home dinner for her tonight hosted by a wealthy banker and prominent political figure, Jaques Lafitte. I am staying home, if I am strong enough to resist Charlotte's pressure to accompany her. She refuses to understand that I am old and feel physically weak, that I have trouble walking. That is why I have avoided socializing. I asked Charlotte last night to excuse me and to send a note to our host apologizing that I will not attend the soirée. I am sure the note has not been written or delivered. I expect my wife will eventually convince me, knowing that Lafitte has been very active in politics, supporting Louis Philippe the Duc d'Orléans to become King of France and supplant Charles X. There are clear indications that another Revolution is brewing, once the weather improves to allow the crowds to be outdoors and cheer a new leader. I have lost count of how many revolutions we have had to suffer for our the lack of serious institutions. Oh that my admired England would model for France this most-needed continuity and stability. Charlotte will use the political situation to convince me how important is for me and for France to participate in what clearly will be a very political evening.

Thinking about Lafitte—whom I owe money—together with the current and constant struggle of power in France, I am aware that most of my books, pamphlets, and speeches have become politically useful for those like me who have defended the same principle for forty years: freedom in everything, in religion, in philosophy, in literature, in industry, in politics. By freedom, I mean the triumph of individuality over the authority that would like to govern by despotism with the support of the masses or the *sans culottes* who demand the right to enslave the minority to the majority. I also use my writings to urge the electors to stop talking about men and vote for principles.

If Madame Staël were still alive, she might possibly validate her opinion of my unstable character merely by observing me in my current state of indecision regarding whether or not to attend a dinner with my wife, especially after having stated a few hours ago that I would not be accompanying her. Charlotte also is aware of how changeable and hesitant I can be, as she has waited to avoid providing an excuse on my behalf to Marine, the wife of Jaques Lafitte.

After a few weeks of gathering material and contemplating the type of text I should write, I have yet to make a decision. Perhaps attending the dinner tonight will provide insight into the direction of current political trends and what might be most effective during these turbulent times. I anticipate that I will be inclined to forego the option of a new memoir that would revisit and possibly distort my past experiences in politics, travel, and love.

* * *

I'm back from the dinner that Charlotte finally convinced me to attend by offering to accompany me to visit my electors in Alsace during the summer, including a trip to Baden, a place where I have many friends. This will bring me the opportunity of enjoying their company once more. It's clear to me that in my current condition, Charlotte's company is necessary for travel. Following her tonight was the right decision after many weeks isolated in my studio, scanning my library for books, letters, anything that I thought could inspire me to write a final book. My desk is full of papers waiting for me in the morning.

During dinner at Lafitte's home, I sat next to Marine, Lafitte's wife, and close to Mme. Gay and Mme. de Gérando. The dinner was luxurious, with a long table for about twenty-four guests, adorned with linen tablecloths and richly embroidered napkins bearing the family seal. The wine and water glasses were modern with a blue hue from the chandeliers. The silver cutlery also had the family seal. The meal included pheasant with colorful feathers and a variety of dark chocolate desserts. We applauded the maître d'hôtel at the end of the dinner. Lafitte seated me near young journalists and law students who respectfully listened to discussions among Left leaders in the Chamber of Deputies and industrialists from various regions.

During the dinner and in the salon drinking cognac, I was asked by several people why not bring together in one volume various essays published at other times in periodic reviews, political books, speeches, and literature as an author of celebrated novellas. I agreed willingly to explore that option, because it seems to be an easier task that will allow me to engage in my work without turning away from more serious political occupations, including visiting my constituency, and taking care of more compelling duties than the scheduled lecture at the Athénée on politics, philosophy or religion. In spite of my increasing weakness, I also also plan to be among the deputies at the autumn sessions at the Chamber to continue my support of liberty of instruction and of a free press.

Now, even though it is late at night and I should be in bed, I find myself unable to sleep. Perhaps I am still energized by the lively conversation during dinner, the encouragement from my friends, and the exceptional Bordeaux served by Charles from one of his vineyards. My mind is preoccupied with plans for tomorrow. I intend to begin by reviewing the numerous pieces of political tracts and literature that I have written, aiming to make selections. I will focus on those closely related to the circumstances that inspired them. I will retain those that appear capable of sparking enduring interest into the future. Additionally, I will assess my drafts and unfinished texts, including unpublished essays. With this framework in mind, I can almost envision the complete collection.

It is late, and tomorrow I embark on a new journey. I express my gratitude to my devoted wife, whose encouragement led me to engage socially this evening, providing me with the opportunity to stay abreast of current affairs firsthand. Tomorrow, my secretary will assist in supplementing the discussions by compiling newspapers and offering his own insights on the day's topics, both from the salons and the streets. With a myriad of thoughts swirling in my restless mind, I extinguish the flickering candle in an attempt to find rest.

* * *

I awoke today brimming with energy and resolved not to linger in bed. Instead, I approached a pleasantly surprised Anne Marie and requested that she prepare the *petit-déjeuner* in the dining room. She was taken aback, yet her face suggested a sense of contentment upon witnessing my early awakening and readiness to commence the day.

I summoned my loyal secretary Jean-Jacques Coulmann, a zealous young liberal from Alsace. I met him some years ago in Mme. Davilliers's Salon when he persuaded me to aid the cause of liberalism by representing Alsace in the Chamber in 1927, two years ago. He is as devoted as a son and as loyal as a disciple. He is also discreet and knows much of my past, including my romances, low moments, and different moods, since he has full access to all my personal letters from my family, my wife, previous lovers, and letters from friends and enemies. He also is aware of my debts, gambling habits, and other defects.

Jean-Jacques will be a great help taking notes and in finding books, newspapers, and any other material in my library that can be used in this project. I hope today we can finish a first draft of a preliminary index with the selection of topics for the new volume, using the old ideas I promoted so vehemently during all those years, together with those that are recently updated and linked to recent political events.

I will require several weeks to compile all the necessary materials, including the chapter titles for the book. Upon presenting the project idea to Coulmann, he enthusiastically extended his support, which I deem essential, given my advanced age. During our discussions, I reminded him of the importance of considering the commitments I have made as a public figure, as well as the criticisms and praises I have received, most of which pertain to my writing, public life, and authored works. I recounted that one of the numerous nicknames bestowed upon me was "constant Constant," a title I proudly embrace, particularly in relation to the ideals of individual freedom and the pursuit of a modern representative government, ideals that have been enduring themes for me since my early political writings following the French Revolution.

A key element to my writing has been my consistent rebuff of the Old Regime, which I saw as a mixture of corruption, arbitrariness, and weakness. Coulmann is aware that I always vehemently defended equality between men and rejected hereditary privilege. He knows, as it is public knowledge, that I abandoned the titles that corresponded to me as a noble from my family roots.

There is an abundance of material for analysis. I trust that Jean-Jacques will be able to extract the essence of my ideas by reviewing the collection of speeches I delivered early in my political career as a member of the Tribunat. These speeches led to my opposition to Napoleon, ultimately resulting in my exile due to their content. Some of these speeches may have been partially written by Mme de Staël.

To show consistency in my defense of individual freedoms, I have asked Coulmann to check the interventions I made many years later, in 1821, at a different representative body as a member of the Liberal Party, during one of the most intense battles between Liberals and Royalists. I made solid arguments I could use in the book, especially my severe criticisms of the proponents of a law which contained what was in all practicality a new form of censorship. I remember the intense debates in the Chamber of Deputies about a new rule that seemed to restrict the last bit of freedom remaining to the nation. My speeches during that time were controversial and were not taken seriously, marking yet another setback in our delicate political system.

A year later my enemies used my arguments in those debates to defeat me in the elections, together with Lafayette and most members of my party. The experience of losing the election was an opportunity to retire from political life and devote myself to thinking about the flaws in a government that depends on the moods of ignorant and indifferent electors. I also saw it as a time to dedicate myself to completing a History of Religions that has been long neglected even today.

Coulmann is taking notes about my actions at that time, in the context of freedom, even without the advantage of the political position I formerly had. With the importance of the several bills, such as those of Primogeniture, and particularly the new laws against Sacrilege, which suppressed certain forms of freedom of religion, I could not afford to be idle or indifferent in the discussion of such vital topics. My secretary, who always shows his good memory, suddenly stopped me from talking to get up from our working table and walk to a pile of books to get my writings for *The Globe* about the case of Colonel Turquet, a bookseller, who was arraigned for impiety because he published the ethical portions of the Evangelists, suppressing the miracles. Coulmann recalled how the ultra-right papers had complained about that unforgettable omission, which they considered equivalent to a denial of the miracles. Their argument was that the law extended tolerance to all faiths, but it contained no provision for a lack of faith, a perfectly sophist argument. As a protector of liberty of thought, whether political or religious, I defended Turquet in my writings, but the courts ignored my arguments, and the poor bookseller was sentenced to imprisonment under the infamous Law of Sacrilege.

Another topic linked to the accusation made against Colonel Turquet is the defense of the educational system of France, which was struggling to rid itself of the influence of ecclesiasticism. I am deeply committed to becoming a vocal advocate for all those who have been wronged by the exclusion of Protestants from positions in the schools and universities of the Departments, which constitutes a direct assault on the fundamental freedom of religion.

Until this day, I persist in actively engaging in debates advocating for individual freedom in areas such as religion, the press, and education. I stand firmly against any form of governmental intervention that seeks to curtail these fundamental rights. History has already borne witness to the immense sacrifices made to establish and safeguard these liberties, and it is imperative that we not allow despots to encroach upon them under the guise of representing an abstract majority, be it the people or the masses.

In the quest for a parliamentary government mirroring the British model together with the pursuit of individual freedom, I have been in the minority. Most of the time against the current, therefore subject to constant personal attacks, particularly accusing me of being a foreigner in France, even if, with the law in hand, I prove that false. I was also subjected to religious prejudices similar to what the Protestants encountered when attempting to enter politics in France. Finally, my dissipated past, passion for gambling, seduction, borrowing from friends and lovers was regularly used to disqualify me. Even if all these defects have an element of truth or interpretation, the notion to make personal an argument about freedom, censorship, or any other issue relevant at the time, was to avoid discussing the essence of that issue. It is a widespread ploy that is used to deflect a serious debate. Another source of attacks I faced in the past, including coming from dear friends like Germaine, was my relationship with Bonaparte, first for supporting him as a Consul, when what I was defending was monarchical legitimism. I also exposed on multiple occasions, in public, the methods that Napoleon was using in order to usurp the sovereignty of individuals.

I have managed to live peacefully without the weight of these notorious weapons being used to affect me personally. My ideas have been under fire, but I staunchly uphold them.

We finished a late lunch and I feel tired after a long morning of hard work. I invited Coulmann to stay, an invitation that was warmly encouraged by Charlotte, who was dressed meticulously in a light blue cotton dress that contrasted with her beautiful dark hair, which was arranged with much art and coquetry. She ordered a splendid lunch with oysters from Brittany that we accompanied with a Grand Cru from Schoenenbourg, which for Coulmann is one of the most delicious and fine wines made in Alsace. We continue with a beautifully presented silver plate with Blanquette de Veau (for the English, French Veal Stew). To finish, our cook's famous creation is Tarte aux Pommes with a lightly burnt crust, holding beautifully arranged apple slices. To make it even more special, we had Armagnac from a very old bottle, reserved for special occasions since it was a present from an influential constituent. The constituent claims that it was from a very old barrel expropriated with a well-aged collection previously owned by a noble or a foreigner during the revolution; it could be more than forty years old. I wonder why Charlotte was planning to prepare such a treat today just for us and Jean-Jacques, a regular guest in our home. She was very vivacious, enjoying herself, playing the role of a great host, almost coquettish.

I am fatigued and need to rest my legs that are failing me. I have no choice but to leave my Secretary and my wife alone to continue with their lively conversation. To be candid, I can envision myself thirty years ago, at the age of Coulmann, who is twenty-nine years my junior, in the company of an older, charming woman, akin to Charlotte, who is wedded to an aging and frail man. It is quite a paradox to contemplate the sentiments of Ambassador de Staël when his wife, my dear Germaine, was alone with me. I am too advanced in years to feel jealousy, and Charlotte is not Germaine. As for Coulmann, I will not vouch for him or any other man.

* * *

It was late last night when Charlotte entered my room to wish me a good night. I pretended to be sleeping since I had no interest in engaging in a conversation about yesterday's lunch with my secretary.

I slowly walk to my studio, after breakfast in bed. Coulmann was already waiting with a selection of speeches from the 1820s, where I bitterly criticized the Government for censoring those like me who had denounced their international inaction. France did nothing to aid Spain against anarchy and turned a blind eye to the massacre of old men, women, and children in Greece. The Government replied to our demands by censoring the press to keep us out of the public view. In the same context, during that time, I was also involved in denouncing the cruelty of the slave trade and, implicitly, the cruelty of slavery, adding my voice to those who decried the indifference of the Government to what was taking place on the island of St. Domingo. Coulmann offered to expand the search for my articles on these issues and to include it in one of the chapters.

* * *

We are making rapid progress in selecting the material for the final compilation of my ideas, to produce one or two volumes. I have informed Coulmann about the significance of including the arguments for individual freedom found in my now-renowned speech "De la liberté des Anciens comparée à celle des Modernes" (On the Liberty of the Ancients Compared with that of the Moderns), which I delivered a decade ago, in 1819 at the Royal Athenaeum of Paris. This essay, which can be viewed as a critique of Rousseau's ideas on collective power, emphasizes that we should never compromise individual liberty for political freedom, asserting that individuals possess rights that society, in various interpretations, must uphold. I also reminded Jean-Jacques that this concise speech was given three decades after the onset of the French Revolution and during the partial restoration of the monarchy.

In that essay, I aimed to present two concepts of freedom: the "old," equated with political freedom, and the "modern," linked to individual freedom. During the Revolution's darkest years, leaders tried to enforce outdated cultural principles of freedom, no longer suitable for the modern era. They believed freedom involved public deliberation on war, peace, alliances, laws, sentences, government accounts, and other complex matters, in front of the people. This collective freedom required individuals to submit entirely to the authority of the assembled crowd, similar to ancient Athens, where society held absolute power over its members. Early revolutionaries overlooked the scale and structure of ancient Greece, attempting to apply it to France with its more complex social system and much larger population.

I drew a comparison as a direct critique of the stance taken by Abbot Mably, known as one of the more extreme demagogues in the Assembly. In accordance with the principles of ancient liberty, he posited that our citizens would be entirely subservient to the whims of a presumed majority, thereby rendering the nation sovereign, at the cost of individual autonomy, all in the name of collective freedom. A similar sentiment can be attributed to Rousseau, who, akin to Mably, conflated the authority of the social collective with the concept of liberty. This, in my view, encapsulates the distinction from the ancients, whose concept of freedom necessitated active engagement from the community, which, in antiquity, was of a modest scale. In our contemporary understanding of freedom, on the other hand, engagement from the community is intertwined with personal autonomy within the framework of law, rather than being contingent on the caprices of an assembly or a mob.

I emphasized to Coulmann the dangers posed by the importance placed on collective action by extremists. A liberal himself, he had witnessed the brutality of the terror years as he observed his father in Strasbourg being detained by a mob and accused of being an enemy of the Revolution by what were then known as "people tribunals." These tribunals sent hundreds of innocent individuals to the guillotine in the name of freedom.

* * *

I am already fatigued from the intense dictation over the past few weeks, where I have covered most of my ideas to provide material for my upcoming book. This book aims to serve as a culmination of my intellectual life. I aspire for it to be a contribution in support of individual freedoms and governments with limited authority that embodies democratic principles, rather than being led by demagogues and self-centered political figures.

I have reviewed the notes and materials compiled by Coulmann, which include our recent extensive discussion on the concepts and themes of my books *Mémoires sur les Cent Jours*, (Memories on the Hundred Days) during which Napoleon and his brother Joseph Bonaparte persuaded me to draft a constitution. This constitution would embody my beliefs in freedom and a moderately progressive government that curbed the growing influence of the clergy and the traditional nobility.

I have to admit, I'd felt proud to be invited by Napoleon to the Tuileries on April 14, 1814. I perceived his reason for calling me was to be useful to him at this juncture of diminished power and conflict. I saw it as a moral duty and an opportunity to promote my adherence to uncompromising Liberal principles. Many friends were surprised to see how easily I changed my view of an old, bitter foe into someone who persuaded me to be transformed, professing a conversion to Constitutionalism. I confessed to Coulmann that I wanted to be involved in a conversion that was real and genuine. The conversation with Napoleon was long and substantial; therefore, I was compelled to make notes after leaving the Palace. I needed to know if the change in this former arrogant giant was real. I did not feel he tried to deceive me either as to his views or as to the evaluation he made about the state of affairs. It was remarkable to not represent himself as chastened by the lessons of adversity. He did not want to claim the merit of having returned to Liberty by inclination. He coldly examined in his own interest, with an impartiality verging on indifference, considering what was possible and what was preferable. Napoleon was candid, saying, as I recall, that his aim was to rule the world and for that he required unlimited power. Looking at my surprised and disappointed face, he stopped to add that he was aware that the people were tired of war, therefore his aim was only to govern France. For that, he said that the only possibility was that a constitution might be a good thing, and he wished to have public discussions, open elections, responsible ministers, a free press, a recitation of all my pet institutions. He claimed that he was aware of the people's desire for freedom.

Coulmann brought me the notebook where I wrote of Napoleon: "I am no longer a conqueror, he said, I cannot be. I know what is possible and what is not. I have only one mission now: to save France." I was almost in tears when our meeting concluded with the following words: "To sustain the nation, the nation must sustain me, but in return it demands Liberty. It shall have it." I interpreted these words as a mandate, an instruction I needed to follow, and that is why I dedicated so much time to drafting a Constitution.

This transformed despot had dismissed me years ago for my defense of freedom in the Tribinat. Now, a defeated yet still influential individual, he admitted that he did not hate Liberty. He honestly acknowledged that he had swept it away when it obstructed his path to power, stating that wars and circumstances needed to be absolute.

Coulmann asked me if it was not my susceptibility to flattery that had won me over, and if that was combined with the cunning of the tactics of one who was, for many, a hero, one whose dramatic reappearance had stunned France and Europe. I had to be honest in explaining the effect of the presence of one whom I thought a great genius. One of the history's most remarkable men was talking to me so intimately and taking me into his confidence.

Probably having the illusion of being able to help in a divided country in chaos, even before Bonaparte sent for me, I had decided to remain in France and accept his leadership. I thought that his period of weakness offered a better chance for liberty. The news of my meeting with Napoleon was badly received by friends and enemies. There was an outburst of abuse from all sides, and floods of letters accused me of having sold myself. The Liberals blamed my acceptance of the Bourbons, the Imperialists reproached me by quoting my previous writings against Napoleon, and the Royalists hated me for my promptness in accepting his reappearance.

My family in Switzerland kept an uncomfortable silence; my beloved Germaine blamed me for falling into a trap. According to a friend, she was so angry that she said it was not her custom to abandon friends in their misfortunes or their mistakes, but in this case she could not forgive me.

Coulmann, after listening and taking notes, suggested using the debates described in my *Mémoires sur les Cent-Jours*, a volume I had decided to publish in 1820 in the form of letters, as a chronicle of another period of political conflict that risked unleashing a civil war in France. I suggested having a whole chapter on constitutional law, using other titles with similar issues, particularly *Réflexions sur les Constitutions, la distribution de pouvoirs et les garanties dans une Monarchie constitutionnelle*. I understand that my book had been translated into Spanish in 1820 and served as a model for the Liberal Party in Mexico to draft their Constitution after their independence.

Coulmann agreed to devise a format that will make explicit my great admiration for the English Constitution and political culture. This may confirm the notion that I am an Anglophile, a term that my enemies used to discredit my arguments for a better government, but it is important to me. I agree to draft at least one of the chapters of the new book dedicated to those principles, to understand from where some of my ideas are borrowed. I prefer the English institutions, like having an aristocratic Upper Chamber (a representative body made by hereditary peerage, unpaid) paired with a popular elected body for balance. I consider that the virtue of the representative system, with checks and balances, is that it allows the participation of the individual and a guarantee of the protection of individual freedom.

My time in Scotland and England, where I learned and acquired a great respect for liberal principles contained in the English Constitution, allowed me to claim without any modesty that nobody in France better understood those principles, giving me an edge in political debates about the future of France's government structure. Mme. de Staël and her father also thought highly of those institutions, which deepened my admiration of the idea of two legislative chambers, one of which should be composed of a strong and enlightened aristocracy, and one responsible for naming and managing the ministers, based on the principle that the King reigns but does not govern. Like Germaine, I believed that a Constitutional Monarchy would fit in better with the political organization of France than a Republic.

* * *

Coulmann patiently listened, took notes, and gathered information from our long days' conversations, and compiled list of titles and all kinds of personal writings. Together, we have produced in less than a year two volumes of a newly printed book. With the help of my wife, we chose the suggestive title: *Mélanges de littérature et de politique* (Interminglings of Literature and Politics), which resonates with the content. Printed in Brussels and London, it was ready just in time since my health is deteriorating rapidly. I am in no condition to work anymore with the energy I had just a few months ago.

After yet another revolution, this time a few months ago, in July 1830, I was appointed President of the Council of State, a relatively obscure and honorary post. I am grateful to my wife who kept her promise to help me pay another visit to my electors in Alsace during last summer, including a trip to Baden. I was able to enjoy the pleasant hospitality of the Coulmanns and other friends, but I was so weak that I needed to delegate to Jean-Jacques, my loyal secretary, the task of addressing the crowds who came to see me, probably for the last time. My faithful Charlotte became an indispensable companion who helped me deal with my fragilities. Most important was her role in socially filling the void

I am leaving behind. I am so glad to see her active, full of life, vindicated by occupying a prominent place in society, which she rightly deserves.

In the last election, I was fortunate to have been elected with a majority for the Liberal Party: 274 deputies versus 143 for the supporters of the Polignac Government. It appears that the motto of my campaign "to save France with the votes" worked in our favor. Upon hearing the news that Charles X had refused to accept the results of the election, risking a revolution, LaFayette and other deputies requested my assistance and active participation in the debates about the future of France. Despite my wife's opinion (she requested that I not leave the bed), I decided to participate in a historic, decisive meeting, leading to the King's deposition and the calling of Duke Louis Philip of Orleans to the throne. This was one of my last legislative initiatives, during which we rejected the censorship laws imposed by the previous Government.

* * *

It is a few months later now and despite my deteriorating health, my sole desire is to be able to assume my usual place among the deputies at the autumn sessions of the Chamber of 1830 after a tumultuous year, in order to advocate for Liberty of Instruction, a Free Press, and the Religion Bill. As a presage, my last days as a public figure this session were disappointing and sad since on that final day in the Chamber, even after we accepted removing references to religion, my project to deregulate printing and bookselling activities, renamed as *Liberty of Instruction of a Free Press*, was rejected by an overwhelming majority. Furthermore, on the same day, I was informed that my membership to the Academy did not proceed as expected, sadly confirming that in politics, being ahead of the times or against the current is not popular among those with power who, with few exceptions, conform to the prevailing trends, changing like the weather without shame merely to align themselves, or retain favor.

Life counterbalances trouble with joy sometimes and I am grateful for the many friends who have visited me in my bedroom while I am immobilized by severe pain. Today, I tried to proofread the final volume of his *History of Religions* but had to stop. I appreciate Coulmann for dedicating much time to listen to my stories and help me complete a book that is an original compilation of ideas and principles that shaped my public life. These include topics like law, government, property, taxation, sovereignty, representation, power, accountability, wealth, poverty, war, peace, public order, and most importantly, individual freedom, freedom of the press, and freedom of religion.

I am holding the hand of my beloved wife, friend and companion, Charlotte, to whom I whisper that I am tired and need to go and sleep. I do not believe it is appropriate to remind her that any religious ceremonies should take place in a Protestant Church. My desire is not only to honor my family and my ancestors, but also to underscore the fact that I belong to a minority group. Like others in similar circumstances, we are often marginalized, mistreated, or constrained in the name of an unseen majority.

Coulmann Recalling His Mentor:
A Sad Goodbye

Seated in my studio, illuminated solely by the flickering light of the fireplace, I am still cold from hours of walking amidst the vast crowd that accompanied Constant to the cemetery. It was an indelible day, one that I am certain Benjamin would have taken pride in for the tribute he received.

I remain deeply sorrowful and melancholic, recalling the moment I escorted Charlotte back to her carriage. Undoubtedly, it must have been a challenging journey for her to return to her now desolate home, devoid of the care and attention she devoted to Benjamin over the last two years. For me, the loss of a dear friend and a remarkable mentor is indeed a profound sorrow, yet it pales in comparison to the anguish his longtime companion is enduring. Charlotte, a resilient woman with a wide circle of friends and a supportive family, will undoubtedly find solace and ease in their company. She is contemplating a return to Germany to establish her residence where her son, Baron Marenholz lives. Despite the trials, she remains youthful and captivating. Benjamin, displaying his inherent generosity and concern for her future, maybe with some remorse for the pain he made her endure during the first two years of marriage, even in his final moments, urged her to embrace a life filled with happiness.

It brings me joy to recall the occasion when I accompanied Benjamin Constant to what would be his final session as a deputy of the Chamber of Representatives on November 26, less than twenty days ago. Charlotte and I attempted to persuade him to remain at home, as he was experiencing back pain and had difficulty walking unassisted. However, he was resolute in fulfilling his duty to advocate for the right of petition in a bill, as he viewed it as a fundamental tool that empowers individuals to defend themselves against humiliations and arbitrary actions by authorities.

I remember him in the carriage on our way back home that day, returning from that emotional session where he had arrived at the hall and received a resounding ovation, one that was repeated with even louder applause when he left the session. Seated in front of him, looking at the people walking in the street, even as the winter sun sets early, I was able to see the saddess of his face, knowing that he might not be able to go back to the Chamber and probably would not have the energy to leave his bedroom again. He told me that day that his only hope was to finish editing the final volume of his book on the history of religion. I tried to reassure him that it was possible, adding that I would be helping him full time. Unfortunately, there is still work I have to do; he did not have the satisfaction of seeing the last volume printed.

From that day until the end, he found joy in receiving his friends, particularly Lafayette among his many other politically liberal colleagues. In contrast, he was keenly aware of the motives of the throng of flatterers who visited him seeking favors following the triumph of the Liberal Party in July. Constant was no stranger to encountering a horde of petitioners, but in those final days, he found them impertinent, avaricious, and self-serving. Fortunately, it was not only his friends who paid him visits; many young people, students, and workers from various trades also came to pay respects. Those last days were a prelude to the extraordinary events that unfolded today at his burial.

For me and other colleagues, today's official State Burial became one of the most significant political events since the July Revolution. Today, Constant was at the center, but he was seen in the context of the triumph of the Liberal Party in the revolution that took place over the summer. To add more solemnity to the occasion honoring Benjamin, the Assembly revisited the previously proposed idea of transforming the church of St. Geneviève into a Pantheon for the burial of the nation's eminent figures. This concept was put forward many years ago during the Restoration period, but no definitive decision was reached, leading to the matter being perpetually pending, since the clericals still regard the Church to be of St Geneviève and oppose the use of the building for any non-clerical purpose.

The procession was scheduled to start from the Temple du Marais, the Protestant church on the Rue Saint-Antoine, where Constant had asked to have final services. There, it was a struggle to decide who should carry the coffin and where to place it. I had to intervene in favor of students to be the ones who carried Benjamin's body on their shoulders to the cemetery of Père Lachaise. It took us more than an hour on foot, an impressive march for a crowd that was not afraid of the snow that had been falling since the morning. There was also a delay at the beginning of the march, since the students tried to turn in the direction of the Seine with the intention of crossing that river to reach the Pantheon, but the police prevented it since the issue of Church status is not yet settled. After a heated dispute followed by a negotiation between those who were carrying the coffin and the authorities led by the mayor, it was finally agreed that we would continue on our way to the cemetery. To calm the people, the authorities announced that they would have the busts of Constant, Manuel, and Foy, the three liberal heroes, placed in Paris City Hall until the question of the Pantheon status was resolved.

I felt honored to be one of several members of the Liberal Party, together with his old colleague and collaborator on *The Mercure*, the famous poet Eusèbe

Baconnière de Salverte, along with the Marquis of Laborde, to pronounce a funeral speech in front of his tomb. The star today was General Lafayette, Constant's closest friend, who had the privilege to be the last person to speak. He gave an eloquent portrait of our dearest Benjamin. As I recall, in his speech, Lafayette mentioned many of Constant's qualities, starting by recalling his education in the best universities in Germany and Scotland, which allowed him to master all the languages and all the literatures of Europe. With tears in my eyes, I vividly recall listening to the somber voice of this national hero giving an account of the ideas and principles that guided Constant's life, particularly to staying permanently loyal to individual freedom; to constitutionalism as a tool of harmony in modern societies; and to a commitment to religious freedom, moderation and rejection of violence. He finalized his speech by raising his voice to underline the iron will our friend demonstrated during his life to always to promote ideas and laws that protect personal liberty and dignity for all, against authoritarian rulers or the violent masses that support them. Lafayette finished his speech, noting Constant's trust in persuasion and dialogue as instruments of reform of societies.

It was a solemn gesture, brimming with emotion, as the light snow began to fall again in the afternoon. We bid farewell to a remarkable individual to whom I owe a great deal for his exemplary conduct and ideas. We had so many relevant conversations about his experiences, both personal and political, making my life richer with a better understanding of the human condition. The image of all the mourners' sad faces, along with our black suits covered in snow, as the women with umbrellas endured the cold while slowly leaving the Cemetery, was a testament to the impact Benjamin had on our lives. His closest friends and even old political adversaries who were present at that solemn moment were deeply affected.

Today was a tumultuous day, confirming Benjamin's reputation for bold and extreme views, which followed him to the end of his life. Against the current, he was ready to change his mind according to what he considered best for France, not for himself. After a dissipated youth, politics became his life. Many people told me, and I agree, that the excitement he felt when participating in a debate was comparable to being in front of a gambling table. He loved to be a Tribune at the Chamber, where he always regained his spirit. He loved the applause, but never as a step towards ambitious designs or wealth like many of his colleagues. It was only for liberty, the sole recompense of his exertions, the sole glory of his days; but he never sacrificed his political opinions for fame or popularity.

Responding to the criticism of his frequent changes in politics made by his opponents and in some cases, his closest friends (including his former lovers, as with Mme de Staël), he explained those dramatic moves in tactics, never on principle. I remember Constant telling me that in politics the shortest distance between two points is not a straight line. To achieve a goal, or get to the desired port, he said, you have to tack to let the wind move you, some times to the left and others to the right, but never forget the direction, your destination, he emphasized, the goal to protect individual freedoms and make governments accountable. That conversation was in the context of the Hundred Years of Napoleon, when my mentor became Councillor of State and wrote the Constitution. He recounted with something of an ironical smile his enemies assailed him calling him as an opportunist, together with Madam Staël, a former political partner who became a vocal anti-bonapartist leader.

My daily routine of walking to Rue d'Anjou No. 17 to meet Benjamin in his bedroom or at the famous Tivoli Baths where he received mineral water treatments to ease the pain in his back, will change. I still have many pending issues to address since he asked me to take care of his will, which includes all of his possessions. I am familiar with the terms of giving his property to his half-brother and sister, but it was clear the instruction was to give priority to the substantial unsettled claims for money loaned to him by Charlotte, to whom he explicitly secured most of his papers and souvenirs. He instructed me to ensure that his wife will be treated well by her in-laws, making me responsible for avoiding the issue of money becoming a situation that could cloud the memory of his life.

But it was the political legacy where his request was particularly emphatic. He instructed me to continue actively promoting his ideas of individual freedom, which as a Liberal myself is an easy task. I have a clear idea of what he meant and what he expected from me. Since I started working for him many years ago, he showered me with all kinds of memorable events and anecdotes of his earlier years, including his romances, frustrations, and his weakest moments when even suicide was considered. His most important concern was to not forget that he never wavered in his advocacy for bringing down every form of privilege, promoting jury trials with citizens and peers; opening professional trades to talent; and expressing popular sovereignty through representative institutions that guarantee the rights of minorities, absolute freedom of speech, freedom of the press, unconditional religious toleration, and the laicization of politics and education. Tomorrow I will start to complete the notes I made when he directly advised me on political issues or ideas.

I also appreciate the trust he expressed in our numerous informal discussions, which were filled with intriguing and very personal anecdotes. These included stories of his motherless childhood, the challenges he faced with tutors, and his distant and aloof father. He also shared his experiences of traveling and learning foreign languages, particularly English, which brought him closer to Lafayette.

Having spent a significant amount of time with Benjamin and Charlotte, it was evident that their marriage was a happy one, despite having a difficult beginning, as was publicly known, given that both had gone through painful previous marriages. Over the past fifteen years, they have shared common interests, with Charlotte being a key figure both personally and politically. In the last two months, Benjamin has become more mellow while speaking to me, as if I were a Priest or a Confessor. He seems regretful for what he has called pain he inflicted upon women, particularly mentioning Mmes Staël and Le Carrière, to whom he owed love and support, and who tolerated what he has described in some detail as indiscretions and frivolity. But his greatest regret was for the actions that embarrassed and hurt Charlotte, who had to endure situations that he considered borderline cruel, a word that he repeated several times. He told me that the marriage with Charlotte took place in 1808 in secret to prevent anyone from knowing he was married. At the beginning of the marriage, they lived apart and he kept Charlotte as a clandestine lover and not as a wife. He was bitter, apprehending his own weakness and incapacity to break with Germaine, who kept Charlotte away, offending her. The situation became so extreme that he described it as devastating to the extreme, asking Anne de Nassau, his closest aunt, to write to de Staël, begging her to set him free. Upon listening to the narrative, I was able to discern the voice of Adolphe, the principal character of the novella that established Constant as a renowned fiction writer.

Fortunately, those years have become distant memories and Charlotte became his true companion, not just the caretaker of his final days. As a harmonious couple, I accompanied them on a visit to my home at Breath a few months ago, taking a political tour to see his loyal constituency in Colmar and Strasbourg for the last time. The Constants's visits have not been easy, as the Royalists have tried to spoil them by publishing negative articles about Benjamin's political past and causing trouble, which has forced the mayors of different cities, the police, and other authorities to intervene. At the end, Benjamin was received as a hero with the roads and streets in the towns full of people wearing national costumes, and Charlotte received enormous bouquets of flowers. One night a crowd serenaded the couple in front of the Hôtel de l'Esprit in Strasbourg, during a sumptuous banquet, clamoring for Benjamin to appear on the balcony. Contradicting Charlotte, who tried to convince him not to go out, once he was there, he was only able to mumble a few words in French and German, asking his wife, who was beside him, to thank the crowd for the enthusiastic welcome. The crowd cheered for their representative, and followed the serenade with fireworks, making Benjamin feel happy. That was a memorable trip, including attending the Sunday services at the Protestant church where the priest praised Constant as the protector of freedom of thought against the assaults of the new clericalism in France.

It is late and I am still processing what was an emotional day, saturated with memories of an historic hero who taught me not to fear to be in the minority and against the current. I feel an enormous responsibility to continue fighting for his ideals, which I fully share. Constant warned me about the difficult times that are ahead. He believes the struggles will continue with new challenges from authoritarian minds that, for power, are ready to erase the liberties that could limit their selfish ambitions. He anticipated that the time of bloody revolutions has not ended. With these ominous thoughts, I must get some rest and try to sleep.

CHARACTERS INCLUDED IN THE TEXT

Louis XV. (King 1715–1774) (February 15, 1710–May 10, 1774)

Jean Jaques Russeau (June 28, 1712–June 6, 1778)

Jacques Necker (September 30, 1732–April 9, 1804)

Duke of Brunswick, Charles William Ferdinand (October 9, 1735–10 November 1806)

Isabelle de Charrière (October 20, 1740–December 27, 1805)

Comte de Clermont-Tonnerre (October 10, 1747–November 10, 1792)

Abbé Sieyès Emmanuel Joseph (May 3, 1748–June 20, 1836)

Baron Erik Magnus Staël (October 25, 1749–May 9, 1802)

Marquis de Lally-Tollendal (March 5, 1751–March 11, 1830)

Charles-Maurice de Talleyrand (February 2, 1754–May 17, 1838)

Louis XVI. King (1774–1793) (August 23, 1754–January 21, 1793)

Comte de Narbonne (May 7, 1755–November 17, 1813)

Charles X Charles Philippe (King 1824–1830) October 9, 1757 November 6, 1836

Maximilien de Robespierre (May 6, 1758–July 28, 1794)

Luise Johanne von Cram (mina) (October 25, 1758–November 23, 1816)

Georges Jacques Danton (October 26, 1759–April 5, 1794)

Malcolm Laing (November 5, 1762–November 6, 1818)

Marie Louise Anne Marie Johannot (December 26, 1763–August 23, 1840)

Madame de Staël (July 22, 1766–Nov 13,1817)

Benjamin Constant (September 25, 1767–December 08, 1830)

Jacques Laffitte (October 24, 1767–May 26, 1844)

Napoleon Bonaparte (August 15, 1769–April 5,1821)

Mme. Marie Françoise Sophie Gay [Nichault de la Valette] (July 1, 1776–March 5, 1852)

Madame Récamier (December 4, 1777–November 05, 1849)

Paul François Jean Nicolas, Vicomte de Barras (June 30, 1755–January 29, 1829)

Jean Joseph Mounier (November 12, 1758–January 28, 1806)

Charlotte Hardenberg [before Mme. du Tertre] (March 9, 1769–March 22, 1845)

Louis Philippe I. "The Citizen King" (1830–1848) (October 6, 1773–August 26, 1859) 85 years

Count Jules of Polignac (May 30, 1780–May 30,1847)

Sir James Mackintosh (October 24, 1765–May 30, 1832)

Stenhal, Marie-Henri (January 23, 1783–February 3, 1842)

Jean-Jacques Coulmann (January 3, 1796–September 9, 1870)

Albertina, Baroness de Staël (June 8, 1797–September 22, 1838)

Charles Augustin Sainte-Beuve (1804–1869)

Alexis de Tocqueville (July 25, 1805–April 15, 1859)

Luis XVIII (July 7, 1815–November 07, 1824)

Benjamin Constant Published Works
(Selection)

Les Chevaliers (1779)
Des reactions politiques (1776)
Des effets de la Terreur (1797)
De la Force du Gouvernement actuel et De la Necessite de s'y rallier (1796)
Fragments d'un ouvrage abandonné sur la possibilité d'une constitution républicaine dans un grand pays (1803–1810)
Principes de Politique Applicables a Tous les Gouvernements (1806–1810)
Le Cahier rouge (1807)
Cécile (1809)
Adolphe (1816)
Mémoires sur les Cent-Jours (1819–1820)
De la liberté des Anciens comparée à celle des Modernes (Speech) (1819)
Appel aux Nations chrétiennes en faveur des Grecs (1825)
De la religion considérée dans sa source, ses formes, et ses développements, 5 vol (1824–1831) 8 years
Discours de M. Benjamin Constant à la Chambre des députés. Tome premier (1827); Tome second (1828)
Mélanges de littérature et de politique (1829)

Bibliography (Selection)

Elizabeth W. Schermerhorn. *Benjamin Constant, His Private Life and His Contribution to the Cause of Liberal Government In France 1767–1830.* Houghton Mifflin Company, Boston and New York, 1925.

Constant, Benjamin. *Constant: Political Writings* Cambridge University Press, 1988.

Kurt Kloocke. *Benjamin Constant: Une biographie intellectuelle.* Droz, Genève, 1984.

The Cambridge Companion to Constant. Assets. Cambridge.org, 17 September 2013.

Wood, Dennis. *Benjamin Constant: A Biography.* Routledge, First ed 1993 Second ed 2011.

Tzvetan Todorov. *Benjamin Constant: la passion democratique,* Hachette, Paris, 1997.

Rosenblatt, Helena, ed. *The Cambridge Companion to Constant.* Cambridge University Press, Cambridge, 2009.

Author's Note

For the Novella, I used direct quotations from Constant's work (my translations). Also, a selection of sources and quotations from letters, and other types of citations are included in Elizabeth W. Schermerhorn's biography.